Rhyme TOWN

Welcome to Rhyme Time Town

Adapted by Natalie Shaw

Simon Spotlight

New York   London   Toronto   Sydney   New Delhi

SIMON SPOTLIGHT

An imprint of Simon & Schuster Children's Publishing Division

1230 Avenue of the Americas, New York, New York 10020

This Simon Spotlight paperback edition December 2020

For information about special discounts for bulk purchases, please contact Simon & Schuster Special Sales at 1–866–506–1949
or business@simonandschuster.com.

Manufactured in the United States of America 1020 LAK

2 4 6 8 10 9 7 5 3 1

ISBN 978-1-5344-8059-9

ISBN 978-1-5344-8060-5 (eBook)

Welcome to Rhyme Time Town!
My name is Cole.
I love to play and make believe
and pounce and leap and roll!

We pretend to be knights.
I say I'm bravest of all.
We go on a quest for dragons or
to save Humpty from a great fall!

My name is Daisy! I'm a pup.
I love to search and rescue.
One day I'll save lost kites just like
Four-and-Twenty Blackbirds do!

Welcome to our barn. Come in! It's filled with toys and books. When it rains, we stay inside and read in cozy nooks.

Humpty Dumpty is my full name.
I'm an egg who climbs quite well.
I like to see how high I can go
but not to break my shell.

I am Humpty's mother, Mumpty.
"Humpty, please stay on the ground!"
I always have some glue to fix
any cracks so he's safe and sound!

This is our home—a fancy nest!
Do you see the red brick wall?
Humpty sits on top of it
and tries hard not to fall!

Hello there! I'm a pig named Jill. Here's my twin brother, Jack. We love to create new objects like a bath on wheels for Ms. Mac!

This is our workshop. Isn't it neat?
The rope brings us water in pails!
We'll never fall down hills again,
unless our cool gadget fails!

Hi there! I am Chuckley Bear.
Mary Mary, want a treat?
I have grapes and melons that are
juicy and ripe and sweet!

Our names are Polly and Molly.
We're chipmunks who like to bake.
We make all kinds of goodies for
our friends in town to take!

See that tea kettle over there?
It is our little diner!
You can sit outside if you'd like.
Could anything be finer?

Hello there. I am Hickory!
Hickory Dickory Dock.
What time does camping start?
Just ask me, the town clock!

Sometimes I can't sleep at bedtime,
and I look for Twinkle Star.
One time I could not find her,
but she didn't go very far!

Town Hall is in the heart of town.
It's also our home, by chance!
We like to have concerts in the park
and teach our teaspoons to dance.

We love to live in Rhyme Time Town!
Please come see us all again.
We hope that you've enjoyed the tour
and that you'll be our friend!